# Rhythm

by **Jackie Azúa Kramer**
illustrated by **Taia Morley**

**Magination Press • Washington, DC • American Psychological Association**

It was the first frost.

Before leaving she whispered to her friend her hopes of good things for her family.

*I hope my father finds work again.*

Winter's rhythm brought
cooking hearty soups
with her father for
her mother's lunch box.

She and her class
drew the tree
decorated in lights
for their classmates
and families that had
moved to find work.

From the tree's twigs and pressed leaves she made holiday gifts.

And in return left breadcrumbs
so the birds would keep it company.

That spring she
returned to discover
a limb torn
from the tree.

She saw its tender
cut and touched her
elbow where there
once was a scab.

She spotted crocuses
hugging the trunk
and skipped home
with a flower pressed
in her pocket.

A perfect gift
from her friend.

Spring's rhythm brought soft breezes
and pale yellow afternoons.

She cupped her ear to hear an army of ants marching into lumpy knotholes.

And under the shady tree she planned adventures with her friend.

When school let out for summer the tree's branches stretched in a wide welcome with wild strawberries nearby.

She kicked off her worn high tops and the ground felt warm and springy.

Her father laughed as sweet, sticky juice rolled down her chin.

Summer's rhythm brought butterflies feeding on asters and milkweed.

She collected ancient
rocks that she tucked
into hidey holes and
she saved nickels
and dimes in her
piggy bank.

tree
fund

Lying under the tree, branches
framed the steely blue sky
with stars for her to wish on.

*I wish I could live here forever.*

Another perfect gift
from her friend.

The days were getting shorter. From the window of her school she read books of brave heroines and saw the top of the tree's orange and red leaves waving hello.

Fall's rhythm brought homemade costumes
as the tree's playful shadows danced in the moonlight.

Her family had Thanksgiving dinner at the Community Meal Center.

The colors of autumn in the canned corn and cranberries they all shared.

Under a tent of blankets with hand-me-down toys she read Aesop's Fables to her sister.

Stories of courage, honesty, and kindness.

The hard winter finally
 melted into spring.

The tree's protective armor,
once a rich, brown bark,
turned a brittle grey.

A crown of branches
lay twisted on the ground.

Yet the tree was surrounded by new life. Ferns, spider webs, and mushrooms.

Delicate leaves sprouted from its remaining branches.

She thought about their friendship... strong, steady, and generous.

And climbed up the tree.

She breathed in the warm air and saw all the things the old tree had seen. Seasons of hope and love. The tree whispered to her of all she could be...

And do.

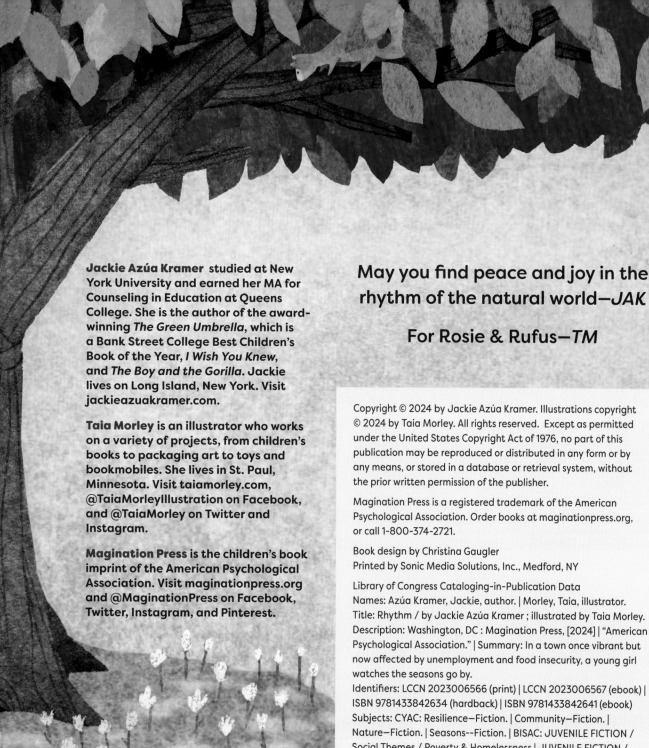

Jackie Azúa Kramer studied at New York University and earned her MA for Counseling in Education at Queens College. She is the author of the award-winning *The Green Umbrella*, which is a Bank Street College Best Children's Book of the Year, *I Wish You Knew*, and *The Boy and the Gorilla*. Jackie lives on Long Island, New York. Visit jackieazuakramer.com.

Taia Morley is an illustrator who works on a variety of projects, from children's books to packaging art to toys and bookmobiles. She lives in St. Paul, Minnesota. Visit taiamorley.com, @TaiaMorleyIllustration on Facebook, and @TaiaMorley on Twitter and Instagram.

Magination Press is the children's book imprint of the American Psychological Association. Visit maginationpress.org and @MaginationPress on Facebook, Twitter, Instagram, and Pinterest.

**Magination Press**
★ ★
Books for Kids From the
American Psychological Association

May you find peace and joy in the rhythm of the natural world—*JAK*

For Rosie & Rufus—*TM*

Magination Press is a registered trademark of the American Psychological Association. Order books at maginationpress.org, or call 1-800-374-2721.

Book design by Christina Gaugler
Printed by Sonic Media Solutions, Inc., Medford, NY

Library of Congress Cataloging-in-Publication Data
Names: Azúa Kramer, Jackie, author. | Morley, Taia, illustrator.
Title: Rhythm / by Jackie Azúa Kramer ; illustrated by Taia Morley.
Description: Washington, DC : Magination Press, [2024] | "American Psychological Association." | Summary: In a town once vibrant but now affected by unemployment and food insecurity, a young girl watches the seasons go by.
Identifiers: LCCN 2023006566 (print) | LCCN 2023006567 (ebook) | ISBN 9781433842634 (hardback) | ISBN 9781433842641 (ebook)
Subjects: CYAC: Resilience—Fiction. | Community—Fiction. | Nature—Fiction. | Seasons--Fiction. | BISAC: JUVENILE FICTION / Social Themes / Poverty & Homelessness | JUVENILE FICTION / Social Themes/Activism & Social Justice
Classification: LCC PZ7.1.A994 Rh 2024 (print) | LCC PZ7.1.A994 (ebook) | DDC [E]--dc23
LC record available at https://lccn.loc.gov/2023006566
LC ebook record available at https://lccn.loc.gov/2023006567
Cataloging-in-Publication Data is on file at the Library of Congress.

Manufactured in the United States of America
10 9 8 7 6 5 4 3 2 1